For Branwen and Oliver

First North American Edition 1992

Published in Great Britain by ABC, All Books for Children,
a division of The All Children's Company Ltd.,
33 Museum Street, London WC1A 1LD, England

Library of Congress Catalog Card Number 91-58069
Library of Congress Cataloging-in-Publication Data
Norman, Philip Ross.
The carrot war / Philip Ross Norman. — 1st ed.
p.   cm.
Summary: When the villainous Hares steal all of the Rabbits' carrots,
the Rabbits come up with a plan involving the Trojan Carrot.
ISBN 0-316-61200-6
[1. Rabbits — Fiction. 2. Hares — Fiction. 3. Carrots — Fiction.]
I. Title.
PZ7.N7854Car   1992
[E] — dc20   91-58609

10 9 8 7 6 5 4 3 2 1

Published simultaneously in Canada
by Little, Brown & Company (Canada) Limited

Printed in Hong Kong

The
CARROT
WAR

Philip Ross Norman

Little, Brown and Company

Boston   Toronto   London

The Rabbits were getting ready for their Midsummer Feast. Little did they know, but two Horrible Hares from Fort Hare were spying on them.

"Come on, Kicker," said Biter. "Let's get back and tell the others what we've seen."

"Open the drawbridge!" shouted
one of the lookouts.

Fort Hare shuddered as the drawbridge crashed down. Kicker and Biter hurried to see Emperor Black Ear deep under the fort. "Well, what did you see?" shouted Black Ear, crushing a radish under his foot. "We've got to get rid of those Rabbits once and for all!" "They're getting ready for their Feast," said Biter. "They're setting up tables and dancing and singing." "And they're getting their carrots ready for picking," added Kicker. "I've got an idea," said Harebrain. "Let's steal all their carrots! That will drive them away." "Brilliant idea, Harebrain!" congratulated Black Ear, jumping up from his throne. "Get everything ready for carrot stealing!"

That evening, when all the baby Rabbits
were safely tucked up in bed, Carbuncle
the Carrot Expert went to check the carrots.
"Tum tee tum, tum tee tum," he hummed,
skipping down to the carrot patch.
Suddenly, there was a loud rustling noise in the
gooseberry bushes.
"The Horrible Hares!" yelped Carbuncle. But
before he could shout "Help!" he was
bundled into a sack.

And with no one to stop them, the Horrible Hares
dug up all the carrots and hopped it back to Fort Hare.

Midsummer Day
dawned bright and clear.
"Yippee, it's party day!" squeaked the little Rabbits.

"Yippee!" shouted Bunlet, the smallest Rabbit of all.
Uncle Bunwun went outside to stretch his legs before
breakfast. But he was soon back. "The carrots are all
gone!" he yelped.

He wasn't wrong. All the Rabbits rushed outside and found huge heaps of earth.

"Moles! We've been attacked by moles!" shouted Bunkum.

"All gone!" sniffed Uncle Bunwun. "All our lovely carrots are gone."

"I've found one!" called Bunlet, spying a carrot in the grass.

"And another!" squeaked Bungler.

Then they found a trail of carrots that snaked down the hill, round a bush three times, and, after a few more wiggles, led straight to Fort Hare. This was awful. It wasn't moles at all! The Horrible Hares had stolen their carrots.

"And they've captured Carbuncle," said Bungler. "I haven't seen him since last night."

What were they to do? The Horrible Hares would never give back the carrots.

"I have a brilliant idea!" said Bungler. "Let's smoke them out. We'll make them give back our carrots!" They made a huge pile of sticks.

Bungler said he was an expert on smoky fires, so he was in charge. Soon there was lots and lots of smoke, and it was drifting in a big black cloud, straight toward Fort Hare.

"Well done, Bungler," said Uncle Bunwun, in a surprised voice.

Just then, the wind started blowing
in their faces. "Oh, dear," said
a worried Bungler. "I think the
smoke is coming back."
It was.

"Run!" shouted Uncle Bunwun to the little ones.

The Horrible Hares didn't even know that
Bungler was trying to smoke them out.

"Well done, my brave Horrible Hares!" shouted Black Ear.
"We'll never see those Rabbits again!" And the sound of
their cheering echoed through the tunnels under Fort Hare.

The Rabbits were very sooty.

Bungler was sootiest of all. He was lost
in the smoke, and couldn't find his way out.

After their bath, the Rabbits were very hungry, but there weren't any carrots.

"Peas and radishes!" said Bunkum. "That's not enough for a growing Rabbit!"

"And we were meant to be having our Midsummer Feast," sniffed Bunter, who was always hungry.

Suddenly Bunlet squawked, "I've had an idea!"

He did lots of drawings to show the others. "There!" he said, proudly.

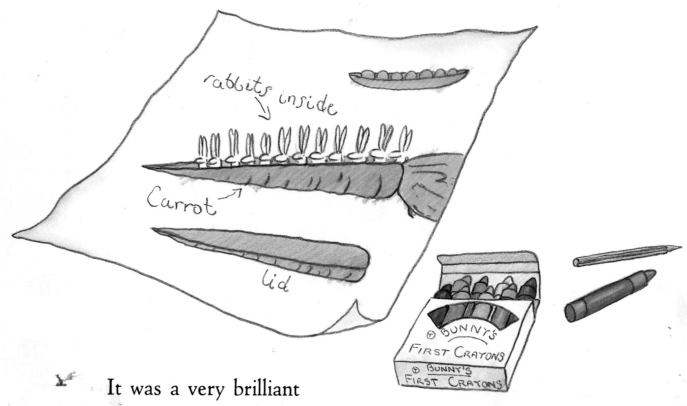

It was a very brilliant idea for such a small Rabbit.

"Let's give the Horrible Hares a huge carrot! They're so greedy, I'm sure they'll let us into Fort Hare."

"But we don't have a huge carrot," pointed out Bunkum.

"Of course we don't," said Bunlet. "We'll make one."

"Hmmm . . ." said Uncle Bunwun, peering
at the drawings. "It just might work."

The next morning they set off for Redwood Forest.
They sawed and chiseled and bashed and hammered, and
soon the tree trunk started to look like a huge carrot.

"OK! Everyone aboard!"
shouted Uncle Bunwun.
As many Rabbits as possible squeezed and
squashed into the carrot. The others had to jump
on the lid to close it. "Now, remember to keep
quiet," Uncle Bunwun whispered
to the Rabbits inside.

And off they
set for Fort Hare.

On the way they met Bungler.
"Jump on," said Bunlet.

"It's a giant
carrot!" shouted Kicker.
"Biter — go tell Black Ear!"

"A giant carrot," said Black Ear. "Sounds tasty. And
how many Rabbits are there?" he asked lazily.

"Ten white ones and a black one, Emperor Black Ear."

"Humph!" And he slurped some carrot wine. "Let
them in!" he commanded. "Steal their carrot! Tie up the
Rabbits and throw them in the dungeons!"

"Open the drawbridge!" shouted Biter to the Hares in charge.

Before the Horrible Hares knew what was happening, the battle had begun!

The battle raged inside Fort Hare. "Quick! Down to the storerooms!" shouted Uncle Bunwun. They all ran down the dark tunnels to the storerooms. "OK," said Bunlet. "Now we've got the carrots, let's save Carbuncle!"

They rushed into the Throne Room, and before Black Ear could even grunt, they had tied him up and poured carrot wine over his head.

But time was running out. They could hear more Horrible Hares rumbling down the tunnels toward them. "This way!" said Bunlet, finding an escape tunnel.

As they scampered over the drawbridge,
Fort Hare groaned and leaned sideways.

That night the Rabbits had a party.

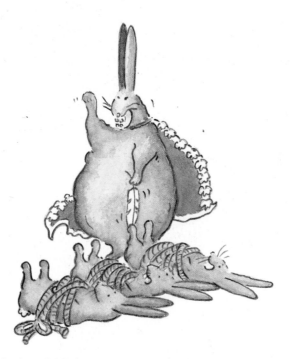

Meanwhile, back at Fort Hare, Black Ear was angry. "We're still the greatest! We'll get those Rabbits yet!"

But the Rabbits were happy bunnies.

Carbuncle was happy because he was safe.

Bungler was happy because he wasn't lost in the smoke anymore.

And Bunlet was happiest of all — he'd not only saved the day; he'd saved the carrots, too.

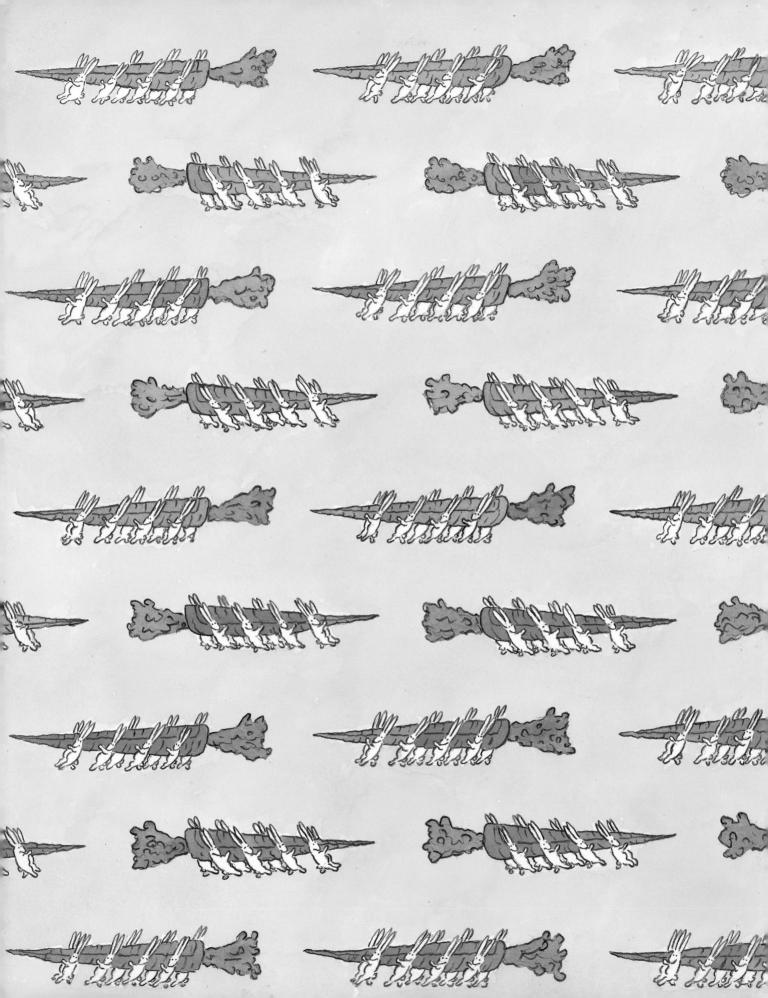